MINI BLUEY

PENGUIN YOUNG READERS LICENSES

An imp... ...York

First 23

First published in the U... ...g Readers Licenses,
an imprint of Penguin Random House LLC, New York, 2024

This book is based on the TV series *Bluey*.

BLUEY ™ and BLUEY character logos ™ & © Ludo Studio Pty Ltd 2018.
Licensed by BBC Studios. BBC logo ™ & © BBC 1996.

Visit us online at penguinrandomhouse.com.

Manufactured in China

ISBN 9780593752814 (pbk)   10 9 8 7 6 5 4 3 2 1 HH
ISBN 9780593752821 (hc)   10 9 8 7 6 5 4 3 2 1 HH

Dad is making breakfast while Bluey sings loudly but beautifully. Bingo reads quietly beside her.

♩♩ OH, WHERE IS MY TOAST? ♫♫♪

"Bluey, can you be as quiet as Bingo for a bit?" asks Dad.

♪♪ NOOOO, I CAN'T! ♫

Meanwhile, Mum is looking for Bluey's missing library book, *Schmurtle the Dirty Turtle*.

"You have to keep better track of your things," Mum tells Bluey.

WHAT ABOUT BINGO? DOES SHE HAVE TO?

"No. Bingo puts her books in a neat pile when she's read them."

"**DING!** Order's up. Cheese and jam on toast," says Dad.

Bluey loves cheese and jam on toast, but Bingo doesn't. She likes peanut butter and banana.

"I'll tell you this for free, my life would be a lot easier if you were both the same," says Dad.

"Bingo! I've got an idea!" says Bluey.

Dad might regret saying that.

Bluey searches through the dress-up basket until she finds **HAIR CHALK!**

She starts painting Bingo blue.
"This is gonna be great!"

Dad finishes off the toast.

"All right, done. Peanut butter and banan—**AH!**"

Now there are **TWO** Blueys!

It's going to be a long day.

"Let's teach you about being me," Bluey says to Mini Bluey.

"I say 'serial' instead of 'serious.'"

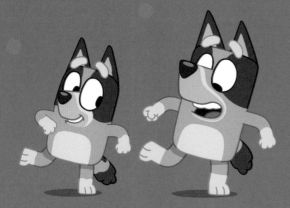

"I like to dance like this . . ."

"And I like to sing . . ."

WOOOOOOORRR! SINGING THINGS!

"I talk *all* the time. It doesn't need to make sense—just noises are fine."

BORT! BORT! BORT!
BORT! BORT! BORT! BORT!
BORT! BORT! BORT!
BORT! BORT! BORT! BORT!
BORT! BORT!
BORT! BORT!
BORT! BORT!
BORT!
BORT! BORT!
BORT! BORT!
BORT!
BORT! BORT!
BORT! BORT! BORT!
BORT! BORT! BORT! BORT!
BORT! BORT! BORT!

"I like to just leave my toys on the ground."

"Isn't it better to tidy them away?"
asks Mini Bluey.

"Nah, it doesn't make much difference."

"I like to ask a *lot* of questions."

MUM, WHAT ARE YOU DOING?

YOU KNOW WHAT I'M DOING BLUEY, I'M—

"But I don't really listen to the whole answer."

"Ooh. And if I see a bum, I give it a little . . ."

BOOM DITTY BOOM.

HEY!

Dad is doing yardwork outside and asks the Blueys to pick up grass clippings. Mini Bluey is ready to help, but . . .

"Whoa, whoa, whoa," says Bluey. "**BINGO** helps Dad. You're **MINI BLUEY** now, and Blueys don't like grass clippings. I'll tell you that for free. Let's find out if he's serial."

EXCUSE ME, BIG FELLA.

"Why do *we* have to put them in the wheelbarrow? They don't belong to *us*."

"Well," says Dad, "you know all that food in the fridge? That doesn't belong to you, either. But if you want to keep eating it, I suggest you get to work."

"Okay, he's serial," says Bluey.

Bluey teaches Mini Bluey to whinge while she works.

Mini Bluey is a fast learner.

"Can I order double Bingos?" asks Dad.

"**NO!** It's double Blueys *forever!*" Bluey yells.

But Dad has other ideas . . .

"May we help you tidy these grass clippings away?"

Big Bingo has a lot to learn.

"I like to pretend I'm hugging a wombat," says Bingo.

"Now put it to bed."

Being Bingo is all about being helpful.

Big Bingo finds the missing library book and gives it to Mum.

"Double Bingo!" says Dad. "I could definitely get used to this."

But that sounds like Dad doesn't want any Blueys at all.

Suddenly the game isn't fun anymore. Upset, Bluey stops playing and runs away.

Bingo doesn't like seeing Bluey sad. "Are you okay?" she asks.

"Mum and Dad want two of yous," Bluey says. "They don't want any of mes."

"It's because I'm annoying. And you're not annoying at all."

"Yes I am! I'm just different annoying. I'll show you!" says Bingo.

She pops some fake teeth into her mouth.

Bluey giggles. She's ready to be Big Bingo again.

"Fowwwow mwe . . ."

Dad is reading the newspaper when . . .

Mum and Dad hide in the cupboard.

"That's it!" Dad shouts through the door of their hiding spot.

"We want **one** Bluey and **one** Bingo from now on. You got that?"

The girls run off.

"Do you think it's safe?" Mum asks.

"I think so . . ."

Close enough.

HOW TO DRAW DAD!

Follow the lines from each step until you finish drawing Dad.

1.

2.

3.

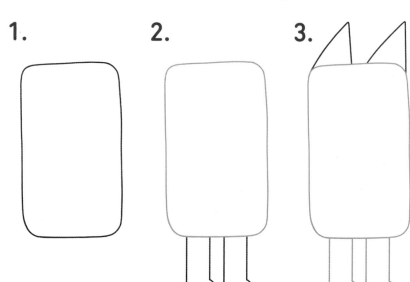

4.

5.

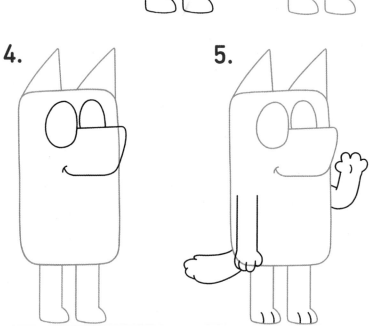

6.

7.

8.

9.

LEARN HOW TO DRAW MUM!

Follow the lines from each step until you finish drawing Mum.

1.

2.

3.

4.

5.

6.

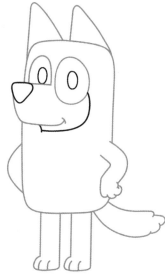

7.

8.

9.

HAIR CHALK HUNT

Help Bluey and Bingo through the maze to reach the hair chalk. Watch out for all the bits and bobs along the way!

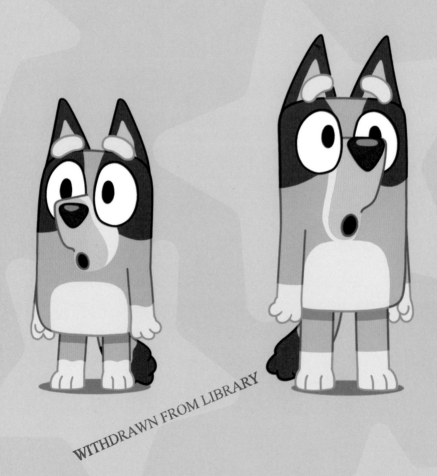